Mary had a Sleepy Sheep

WRITTEN BY
Julia Dweck

ILLUSTRATED BY
Wilson Williams, Jr.

D1402456

For my husband, Sheppard,
who shares my dreams
and helps me achieve them
by the light of day. – J.D.

For my sister Wenona (Wendy),
who was a super deep sleeper
and could sleep through anything
but would always come and get in bed
with me when she was scared at night.
Love ya' sis! – W.W.

Young Mary had a little lamb,

His name was **Sheppard Sheep**,

And everywhere that Mary went

That sheep was sure to **Sleep**.

He followed her inside one day
And lay down on her **Bed**.
It made her mother **scream** and **yell**,
and this is what she **said**.

"Now Mary, get that **SHEEP** outside."

This made poor Mary **SAD.**

Her Mother **kicked** him out of **Bed**,

and she was steaming **mad**.

So Mary bought a little book

With ways to stay **awake**.

Since Sheppard always fell asleep,

Twas **more** than she could **take**.

Sheep Sleep
8 easy ways to wake your Sleepy Sheep

When Mary bought him dancing shoes.

They **SAMBA'D** through each **CHORD**.

Yet Sheppard tangoed, waltzed, and bowed,

And sleepwalked as he **SNORED**.

Mary turned the lights on **Bright**

She'd little left to **lose.**

But suddenly the lights blew out,

And Sheppard took a **snooze**.

Now Mary turned the water on,
She **SPLASHED** it from the **hose**.

As soon as Sheppard lapped it up.

He slipped into a **DOZE**.

So Mary cooked some **spicy** food —
Fiesta made **for two**.
And as he slurped the chili down,
Siesta'd through **each chew**.

Mary turned on **funny** shows,
and laughed through quite a number.
When Mary turned to laugh with him,
he'd fallen into **Slumber**.

Then Mary found a feather quill,

And lathered shaving **cream.**

She tickled him until he sneezed,

And fell back in his **Dream.**

When Mary turned the heater off,
It made poor Sheppard **freeze**.
He lay across his snow-topped bed,
And caught a few more **ZZZZ'S**.

Then Mary **Blew** a large French horn.
And played a marching **Song**.
Although her sheep plugged both his ears—
Asleep he "baahed" **along**.

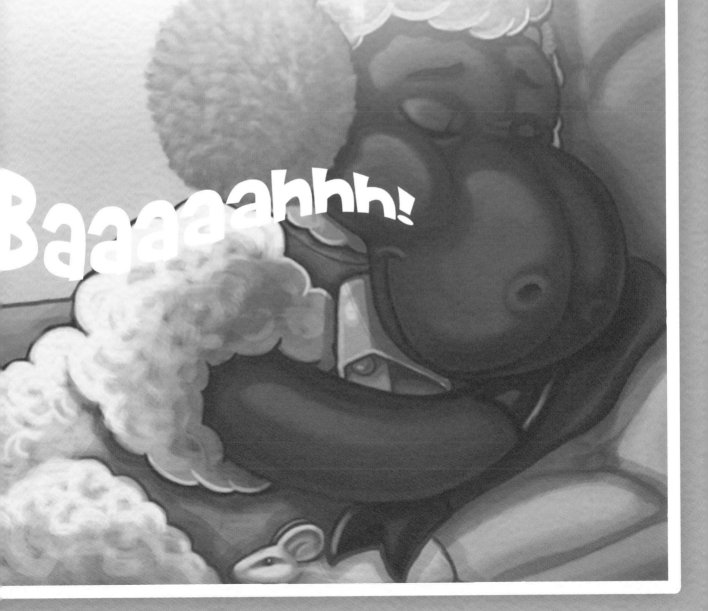

So Mary **STOPPED** and scratched her head,

while Sheppard slept 'till **noon**.

She'd somehow wake that sleepy sheep,

and she would do it **soon**.

Then Mary thought how humans **sleep** when they are feeling **wired**.

They count a bunch of leaping sheep until they feel too **tired**.

So Mary taught her sheep to **count,**
from numbers, one to **ten.**

Instead of counting little sheep,

Her Sheppard counted **men**.

Mary's sheep is **WIDE**-awake,
WIDE-awake,
WIDE-awake

Now that her sheep's **WIDE** awake,
it's **MORE** than she can **take!**

Julia Dweck

is a gifted specialist and children's author who loves writing stories for children, including *Where Are the Dinos?* illustrated by Bob Ostrom.

Sheppard Dweck is Julia's husband and inspired Mary's very sleepy sheep. To help Julia sleep through Sheppard's loud snoring, she wears earplugs while she dreams up new ideas for exciting children's stories each night!

Wilson Williams, Jr.

is the illustrator of many books for children, including *A Perfect Pet for Peyton* written by Gary D. Chapman and Rick Osbourne.

To help Wilson catch some z's, he loves to exercise his imagination before going to sleep. Wilson does this by listening to music, sketching or reading a favorite book!

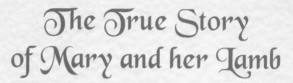

The True Story of Mary and her Lamb

Mary Had a Sleepy Sheep is a retelling of the original poem, *Mary Had a Little Lamb.* Mary Sawyer lived in Sterling, Massachusetts and attended the Redstone Schoolhouse. She actually had a little lamb, which her brother urged her to bring to school. *Mary Had a Little Lamb* was published in 1830, as a poem by Sara Josepha Hale. If you visit the town of Sterling, you'll find a statue of Mary's little lamb in the town center.

Mary had a Little Lamb

Mary had a little lamb,
its fleece was white as snow;
And everywhere that Mary went,
the lamb was sure to go.

It followed her to school one day,
which was against the rule;
It made the children laugh and play,
to see a lamb at school.

And so the teacher turned it out,
but still it lingered near,
And waited patiently about,
till Mary did appear.

"Why does the lamb love Mary so?"
the eager children cry;
"Why, Mary loves the lamb, you know,"
the teacher did reply.

HEY!

I could sure use your help.
My cat has a favorite toy mouse
that he hides all the time.
Can you help me look back through
the book and find where he's hidden it?

There is a toy mouse hidden
on every page of the story!

Below are two images. Look at the one on the left and see

Sheep Activity Page

how many things are different from the one on the right.

Mrs. Dweck's Favorite Fun Sites

Each of the following sites is a free web resource
that offers a fun learning activity.
Remember to get a parent's permission before
visiting any sites on the internet.

Blissful Blabbers

Are you a talented actor? Blabberize is a fun site where you can
upload images and make them talk or "blabber." Create nursery
rhyme blabbers. Upload an image, make it blabber, and record
your voice sharing a dramatic recitation of your favorite nursery
rhyme.

www.blabberize.com

Creative Cartoonist

Are you an artist who loves cartooning? Visit Toondoo to create
your own nursery rhyme comics. You can even make a ToonBook
based on an original nursery rhyme that you create yourself.

www.toondoo.com

Awesome Author

Are you an amazing author? Use Mixbook to create an online book with your own funny versions of classic nursery rhymes and photos. You can view and present your book online like a slide show.

www.mixbook.com

Dazzling Designer

Are you interested in learning programming? Scratch was developed by MIT as "a programming language that makes it easy to create interactive art, stories, simulations and games—and share those creations online." I just thought it was fun. Can you create a Mary Had a Sleepy Sheep game to challenge your friends?

scratch.mit.edu